PENGUIN POETS

LAST WALTZ IN SANTIAGO

Born in Argentina in 1942, Ariel Dorfman is a Chilean citizen. A supporter of Salvador Allende, he was forced into exile after the coup of 1973. His most recent novel, *The Last Song of Manuel Sendero*, was published to stunning reviews. "The conception is brilliant; the whole novel is fraught with wonderment," said *The Washington Post*. Ariel Dorfman is also the author of *How to Read Donald Duck, The Empire's Old Clothes*, and *Widows*, and his work has been translated into twenty languages. He is a regular contributor to *The New York Times*, the *Los Angeles Times*, *The Nation*, and the *Village Voice*. Each fall he teaches as a visiting professor at Duke University.

LAST WALTZ IN SANTIAGO

ALSO BY ARIEL DORFMAN

ARIEL DORFMAN

LAST WALTZ IN SANTIAGO

AND OTHER POEMS OF EXILE AND DISAPPEARANCE

TRANSLATED BY
EDITH GROSSMAN
WITH THE AUTHOR

PENGUIN
BOOKS

PENGUIN
Published by the Penguin Group
Viking Penguin Inc., 40 West 23rd Street, New York, New York 10010, U.S.A.
Penguin Books Ltd, 27 Wrights Lane, London W8 5TZ, England
Penguin Books Australia Ltd, Ringwood, Victoria, Australia
Penguin Books Canada Limited, 2801 John Street, Markham, Ontario Canada L3R 1B4
Penguin Books (N.Z.) Ltd, 182–190 Wairau Road, Auckland 10, New Zealand

Penguin Books Ltd, Registered Offices: Harmondsworth, Middlesex, England

First published in simultaneous hardcover and paperback editions by Viking Penguin Inc.
1988
Published simultaneously in Canada

Part One of this book was first published as *Missing: Poems by Ariel Dorfman*
by Amnesty International British Section.

This collection was first published in Chile by Sinfronteras as *Pastel de Choclo*.

LIBRARY OF CONGRESS CATALOGING IN PUBLICATION DATA
Dorfman, Ariel.
Last waltz in Santiago and other poems of exile
and disappearance.
(Penguin poets)
Translation of: Pastel de choclo.
I. Grossman, Edith, 1936– . II. Title.
PQ8098.14.07A24 1988 861 87-21208
ISBN 0 14 05.8608 3 (pbk.)

Printed in the United States of America by
R. R. Donnelley & Sons Company, Harrisonburg, Virginia
Set in Electra

CONTENTS

PART 2

POEMS I WASN'T GOING TO SHOW TO ANYBODY

PART 3

UNDERTOW

EPILOGUE

AUTHOR'S NOTE

To translate a poem is never easy. In this collection, two words stubbornly resisted an English-language equivalent. It is significant that one is a word of horror and the other a word of hope—two inextricably linked experiences in today's Latin America.

The words are *pau d'arara* and *compañero.*

I first heard about *pau d'arara* in the 1960s. It was a method of torture used in Brazil, but exported later on to other equally unfortunate lands. The victim, hands and feet tied together, is strung up naked on a horizontal stick. To describe what then happens would require words that I prefer to leave unspoken.

Compañero, a man, or *compañera*, a woman, could be rendered as *mate, friend, comrade, companion;* but none of these has the unique resonance of the Spanish. If you look at the origins of the word, a *compañero* is one with whom you share bread.

Too often, it is those who try to make the world into a place where we could all be *compañeros*, it is those dreamers of the future, who wind up on the *pau d'arara*.

ARIEL DORFMAN
June 1987

PART 1

TO MISS, BE MISSED, MISSING

FIRST PROLOGUE: SIMULTANEOUS TRANSLATION

I'm not so different from the interpreters
in their glass booths
at endless international conferences
translating what the peasant from Talca
tells about torture
repeating in English that they put him on the cot
stating in the most refined and delicate French
that electric shock produces lasting transmissible effects
finding the exact equivalent for rape by dogs
pau d'arara I insulted the murderers
finding a phrase without emotion
that describes exactly the sensation
—please forgive any rhymes or rhythms you may find—
when the wall is at your back
and the captain begins to say the word fire,
trying to take the melodrama out of the sentences
trying to communicate the essence and the feeling
without giving in to the dark cloying current
of what they are really saying
they were torturing my son in the other room
they brought back our compañero unconscious
they put rats inside our compañera it's God's truth.
Not so different from them
with their voices their dictionaries their notes their
culture their going back home
in Geneva in New York in the Hague,
an intermediary, not even a bridge,
simultaneous translation for good pay
because we are specialists

and the incredible thing is that in spite of us
in spite of my river of interpretations and turns of phrase
something is communicated
a part of the howl
a thicket of blood
some impossible tears
the human race has heard something
and is moved.

RED TAPE

find out check information go to the
police station then to regimental headquarters hire lawyers
sign petitions begin to knock on doors talk to relatives
call up old girlfriends find people with influence petition
in court talk to released prisoners listen to rumors
petition again appeal attend meetings with other
parents make copies of the photograph talk to a foreign
reporter mail another letter wake up in the
middle of the night when a car stops in front of the house
hear the news that your fiancée is getting
married re-read your composition book from junior
high petition the supreme court look at the street

just
to be able
to bury your body,
to have a place
where your mother
can go with
flowers
(you liked chrysanthemums
but they cost so much)
on Sundays
and All Souls'
Day.

SHE'S LOSING HER BABY TEETH NOW

who's that who's that man
with Uncle Roberto?

oh, honey, that's your father

why doesn't daddy ever come
to see me?

because he can't

is daddy dead?
is that why
he never comes home?

and if I tell her that daddy
is alive
I'm lying
and if I tell her that daddy
is dead
I'm lying

so I tell her the only thing
I can
that isn't a lie:

daddy never comes home
because he can't.

HOPE

FOR EDGARDO ENRIQUEZ, SR.
FOR EDGARDO ENRIQUEZ, JR.

My son has been
missing
since May 8
of last year.

They took him
just for a few hours
they said
just for some routine
questioning.

After the car left,
the car with no license plate,
we couldn't

find out

anything else
about him.

But now things have changed.
We heard from a compañero
who just got out
that five months later
they were torturing him
in Villa Grimaldi,
at the end of September
they were questioning him

in the red house
that belonged to the Grimaldis.

They say they recognized
his voice his screams
they say.

Somebody tell me frankly
what times are these
what kind of world
what country?
What I'm asking is
how can it be
that a father's
joy
a mother's
joy
is knowing
that they
that they are still
torturing
their son?
Which means
that he was alive
five months later
and our greatest
hope
will be to find out
next year
that they're still torturing him
eight months later

and he may might could
still be alive.

CORN CAKE

My old lady had nothing
to do with any of it.

They took her
because she was our mother.
She knew nothing
I mean
nothing about nothing.

Think about it.
Even more than the pain
think how amazed she was.
She never even knew
there were people
like them
in this world.

Almost two and a half years
and she hasn't come back.
They came into the kitchen
and left the kettle boiling
on the stove.
When the old man came home
he found the kettle
dry
steaming on the stove.
Her apron was gone.

Think how she must have
looked at them

for two and a half years,
how she must have . . .
think about the blindfold
coming down
                    over her eyes
for two and a half years
and those same men
who shouldn't be in this world
coming toward her
                    again.

She was my mother.
I hope she never comes back.

HIS EYE IS ON THE SPARROW

Forgive us, Lord, for sending
this petition
but we have no place else to turn.
The Junta won't answer,
the newspaper makes jokes and is silent,
the Court of Appeals will not hear
the defense appeal,
the Supreme Court has ordered us to
cease and desist,
and no police station
dares
receive
this petition
from his family.

Lord, you who are everywhere,
    have you been
    in
    Villa Grimaldi
    too?

They say nobody ever leaves
the Colonia Dignidad,
or the cellar on Londres Street,
or the top floor of
the Military Academy.

    Have you?

If you have,
if you really are everywhere,
please answer us.
When you were there
did you see our son
Gerardo? Lord, he was baptized
in your church,
Gerardo, the most rebellious, the sweetest
of the four.
If you don't remember him
we can send a snapshot
the kind you take in the park
on Sunday,
and the last time we saw him,
right after supper,
that night when they knocked
on the door,
he was wearing a blue jacket
and faded jeans.
He must still be wearing them now.

Lord, you who see everything,
have you
seen him?

TWO TIMES TWO

We all know the number of steps,
compañero, from the cell
to that room.

If it's twenty
they're not taking you to the bathroom.
If it's forty-five
they can't be taking you out
for exercise.

If you get past eighty
and begin
to stumble blindly
up a staircase
oh if you get past eighty
there's only one place
they can take you,
there's only one place
there's only one place
now there's only one place left
they can take you.

LAST WILL AND TESTAMENT

When they tell you
I'm not a prisoner
don't believe them.
They'll have to admit it
some day.
When they tell you
they released me
don't believe them.
They'll have to admit
it's a lie
some day.
When they tell you
I betrayed the party
don't believe them.
They'll have to admit
I was loyal
some day.
When they tell you
I'm in France
don't believe them.
Don't believe them when they show you
my false I.D.
don't believe them.
Don't believe them when they show you
the photo of my body,
don't believe them.
Don't believe them when they tell you
the moon is the moon,
if they tell you the moon is the moon,

that this is my voice on tape,
that this is my signature on a confession,
if they say a tree is a tree
don't believe them,
don't believe
anything they tell you
anything they swear to
anything they show you,
don't believe them.

And finally
when
that day
comes
when they ask you
to identify the body
and you see me
and a voice says
we killed him
the poor bastard died
he's dead,
when they tell you
that I am
completely absolutely definitely
dead
don't believe them,
don't believe them,
don't believe them.

ANNIVERSARY

And every September 19th
(soon it will be four years,
can so many years have gone by?)
I will have to ask her again
if there is any news,
if they have heard anything,

and she will say no, thank you very much,
I appreciate your concern,
but her eyes will keep saying
wordlessly
what they said the very first time
(soon it will be three years—
how is it possible?)
no, thank you very much,
I appreciate your concern,
but I am not a widow
so stay away from me,
don't ask me for anything,
I won't marry you,
I am not a widow,
I am not a widow
yet.

IDENTITY

What did you say—they found another one?
—I can't hear you—this morning
another one floating
in the river?
talk louder—so you didn't even dare
no one can identify him?
the police said not even his mother
                        not even the mother who bore him
                        not even she could
they said that?
the other women already tried—I can't understand
                                                what you're saying,
they turned him over and looked at his face, his hands
                                                they looked at,

                        right,
they're all waiting together,
silent, in mourning,
on the riverbank,
they took him out of the water
he's naked
            as the day he was born,
there's a police captain
and they won't leave until I get there?
He doesn't belong to anybody,
you say he doesn't belong to anybody?

            tell them I'm getting dressed,
                        I'm leaving now

if the captain's the same one as
last time
he knows
what will happen.
that body will have my name
my son's my husband's
my father's
name
I'll sign the papers tell them
tell them I'm on my way,
wait for me
and don't let that captain touch him
don't let that captain take one step closer
to him.

Tell them not to worry:
I can bury my own dead.

I JUST MISSED THE BUS AND I'LL BE LATE FOR WORK

I'd have to piss through my eyes to cry for you
salivate, sweat, sigh through my eyes,
I'd have to waterfall
I'd have to wine
I'd have to die like crushed grapes
through my eyes,
cough up vultures spit green silence
and shed a dried-up skin
no good to animals
no good for a trophy
I'd have to cry these wounds
this war
to mourn for us.

FIRST WE SET UP THE CHAIRS AND THEN WE PUT THE BLANKETS ON TOP. NOW WE HAVE A NICE LITTLE HOUSE JUST FOR US. NOW LET'S PRETEND THAT I'M THE DADDY AND YOU'RE THE MOMMY AND WE TALK LIKE THEY DO WHEN THEY THINK WE'RE ASLEEP. OK?

If they come for me at night . . .
Then I pretend I'm the mommy who knows what to do—
Wait until morning
and go see the lawyer don Alfonso.
And if they come during the day . . .
Then I let Leandro know
through the party.
Just make sure they're not watching you.
Just make sure they're not watching me.

And if they take you away too?
That will never happen.
But if they decide to take you away
too?
Then make believe I'm the mommy who says
that the oldest,
Juan,
will know what to do.

Now they talk about us.
They talk about us?
About you and me and Juan,
don't you remember?
But I always
fall asleep.

What if they take the children?
That's what you have to ask
if you're the mommy.

That's what I have to ask?
What if they take the children?
That's what I ask, right?
Then I pretend to be the daddy
And I start to yell and say
don't ask stupid questions,
not even they would do that.
And if I'm the mommy
what did I say then?
What do I say then?

You don't say anything.
You just stay quiet.
Just like now.

THE OTHER COMPAÑEROS IN THE CELL ARE ASLEEP

You go into the one bedroom
                                        in the house
and you don't turn on the light
so you won't wake up
                                the children.

You take off your clothes in the dark
and stretch your hand under the blanket
and feel the warm sleep
                                  of the youngest,
the daughter I don't know,
the daughter born afterwards.
You stand there, naked,
you don't get into bed,
your eyes are open
almost touching the breathing
                                        of our children.

Tomorrow you have to go to the prison
and they will tell you no,
tomorrow you have to look for work,
tomorrow you have to ask for credit
and always no, the same no,
come back
        tomorrow
but hush, let's not cry
—don't be afraid

you can
they're all asleep—
the dark is full
of children.

I DON'T KNOW WHERE HE LIVES. WE AGREED TO SEPARATE BECAUSE WE WEREN'T GETTING ALONG. THE CHILDREN ARE WITH ME AND ONCE IN A WHILE HE SENDS ME A LETTER. NO RETURN ADDRESS. THAT'S ALL I CAN TELL YOU

As for me
I have to sleep
with your memory
to find you
        and sometimes
        if I'm lucky
        you'll come back
                later
        in what are generally
        my dreams.

As for the secret police you can be certain
                they don't look for me with dreams
        and if they find me
        one uncertain night
                —the sound of brakes
                of men who jump from
                moving cars
                and footsteps coming closer
                will awaken me—
        you won't know
        you won't be here
        to protect me
        to look for me
                —they'll tell you they haven't
                arrested me—
        later.

SOFT EVIDENCE

If he were dead
I'd know it.
Don't ask me how.
I'd know.

I have no proof,
no clues, no answer,
nothing that proves
or disproves.
        There's the sky,
        the same blue
        it always was.
But that's no proof.
Atrocities go on
and the sky never changes.
        There are the children.
        They're finished playing.
        Now they'll start to drink
        like a herd of wild
        horses.
        Tonight they'll be asleep
        as soon as their heads
        touch the pillow.
But who would accept that
as proof
that their father
is not dead?
The madness goes on
and children are always children.

Well, there's a bird
—the kind that stops
in mid-flight
just wings in the air
and almost no body—
and it comes every day
at the same time
to the same flower
just like before.
That doesn't prove anything either.
Everything's the same as it was the day they took him
away

as if nothing had happened
and we were just waiting
for him to come home from work.
No sign, no clue,
nothing that proves
or disproves.

But if he were dead
I'd know it.
It's as simple as that,
don't ask me how.
If you were not alive
I'd know it.

NUPTIALS

every morning when I open my eyes
you die again
you die again
and in my dreams they've just
killed you
I don't find you again alive
understand?
there's nothing in the world I can do
to stop them in my dreams from

every Sunday I put on my wedding suit,
I go to see your father,
we open the album,
wine and biscuits the pleasant phrases back
and forth,
we both know that some day you'll come back,
but the face they kill when I open my eyes
and the face that breaks apart every night
is never in those photos, understand?
that your father keeps intact.

must I lose you even in my dreams?
let me have the night at least
for dreaming of you alive, at my side, in the dark,
your face quiet and warm like an echo
I touch far away in the album,
the night for trying on memories and bodies
mother, grandmother, honeymoon,
memories and bodies and photographs and nights

that you'll never be able
understand?
to have.
then afterwards
I open my eyes
my eyes at dawn
and what they did to you in my dreams
they've done to you already
they've done to you already
one last final time.
I begin to live, begin to breathe
for two, for three, for six, for all
our children you will never bear.

in my dreams and at dawn
in that other place
you scream and you
scream
and there is nothing
understand?
I can do
to make you
stop.

SOMETIMES I SEE THE CITROEN. THEY'VE CHANGED THE LICENSE PLATES AND REPAINTED IT. BUT I LEAVE THE COURTHOUSE AND I SEE IT THERE WITH THE SAME MEN AND THE MOTOR RUNNING

We almost ran him over.
The dog
ran into the road
so suddenly
that Sunday
while we were singing
the five of us singing on the way to Melipilla
because it was Sunday
we were having a picnic
and the sun was shining so bright.
The dog
appeared like a living shriek
a kick in the throat
little earth color maybe coffee I don't remember
and he ran in front of us
as if the devil were chasing him
or as if we had swallowed
a very hard bone.
A screech of tires
watch out for the dog
watch out for
and we hit
a tree
before we stopped.
You got out to look at the car.
And you smiled.
Come see, everybody.
Lucky mutt, you said.
Not a scratch.

And you smiled
and you smiled
until the children stopped
crying.
The fender's ruined I said just to say something.
A dent like an eye of metal
twisted like white lips.
Where did those words come from
on that nice sunny day?
You shook your head like a big friendly lion.
The fender? That's easy to fix.
And you spoke to them lifting your hands
like an old-fashioned preacher at the top of a mountain.
Children, the only thing in this world you can't fix
is taking the life of something that by some miracle
breathes.
And then
you smiled.
But maybe because it made us sad to see the
cold open wound
in the dark tree bark
we didn't sing that song for the rest
of the trip.

We never had time
to fix the fender.
In two days, it was Tuesday,
they came for you.
As they left the house
they saw the car on the street.
We'll take the Citroen too,
they said,
just to keep him company.

On the way back,
it must have been ten and the children were asleep,
you carefully stopped the car at that place near Melipilla.
We couldn't see but it was the same place.

We couldn't see as if someone had
covered our eyes
with black cloth.
        But you opened the door
and we listened to the frogs croaking
                    in a nearby pool
and I saw a half moon
                    growing
          between stars
          and a ripe sky.
You searched with the flashlight among bushes
                                        and trees
you crouched among the stones on the road.
The trucks passed by
like a shout of screaming lights
                    and made the Citroen shake
while all I could see of you
                    was the flashlight
like the distant window of a train going
                              back and forth
through the night.
                    When you got back in,
                         you sighed with relief.
                    We didn't hit the dog.
                         I was worried about that
                    but there's no mark, no stain.
                    Lucky mutt, you said.
                         Not a scratch.
All the way home
you whistled the song slowly
slowly so the children wouldn't hear you,
softly accompanying their dreams from
                         a distance that was full,
you were whistling the song
that had been cut off
                    as suddenly
                         as a living shriek
that Sunday morning

so sunny and bright
and your face was in shadow
but I know that you were smiling
in the deepening dark.

COST OF LIVING

FOR ISABEL LETELIER

and now they want to kill him by decree
and make me start acting like a widow
and not keep searching the streets
showing his photograph, they say, to every passerby.

as if he had been killed in a distant war
they suggest I ask for a pension
they suggest I ask for money
to buy schoolbooks for my children.
That's what they want:
                    for me to put away his photograph calmly
next to the photograph of my parents,
and go out to buy milk
                    every day
with the money from the pension.

but they don't seem to understand.
I would like to put away his photograph calmly,
it's true
          that's what I want to do
          and that's what I will do
and it's not that we have plenty of schoolbooks
                                        in this house,
or even food to spare.
but there's something else
                    something else before I put away the
                                        photograph
and I wonder if they can understand.
it's nothing unusual,

it's quite normal:
I just want to see the face of the man
of the man who killed him,
not for revenge, I'm not angry.
I just want to see the face of that man
or the face of the man
who bought the bullets
that killed him.

It's so simple after all,
even a child could understand.
those schoolbooks
let there be no doubt about it
I'll buy those books

that's what I want to say
to the man who killed him.

he won't buy milk for my children.
he will not buy milk
for my children.
that's what I want to say
and let him try to understand.
I want him to understand
while I look him in the face
while I keep on searching
—calmly—
the face of the man who killed him.

CORRESPONDENCE

To all those who voted for Salvador Allende in Chile's last free presidential election, on September 4th, 1970.

for many days
after
after they came for you
letters kept coming
for weeks
for months
letters that I've saved
from people who knew you.

Then people found out
they always find out
the letters stopped coming
and the visits dwindled away
to a trickle
after a rain-
storm.

I've thought about sending them back
unopened unread
with a note:
My daughter Carolina regrets
she is unable to respond.
that's how you say these things.
that's how I learned to say them.
but they stick
to my hand
I don't want to mail them
your friends are inside
the ones you didn't bring home,

the people who were your friends,
if I only knew what they are saying to you
what they are saying and what they said
those people
I never knew
and who were different from me,
but one doesn't open other people's mail.
that's a basic rule
of good breeding.

there's someone, though, who keeps writing.
every year there's a card
dated September 4th
and underneath an illegible signature.
I will always remember
says the card
that September 4th
until the day I die.
and then the illegible signature.
who knows who it's from
because toward the end
we didn't talk very much
you wanted to move out.
for political reasons, for other reasons,
you called me old-fashioned
you said I didn't understand you.
You used to tell me everything, you'd come to me with
all your troubles
and little by little you locked yourself in
and I heard the key
in the door of your room
and we didn't talk anymore.
I may be very old-fashioned
but I knew it would come to no good,
no good,
I told you and you wouldn't
you wouldn't
listen.

so all I know
about the young man
is that after so much time
he still sends you
the same words of love
every year.

don't worry.
if he ever visits you,
if he comes for you some day,
don't worry,
I'll know what to do.
when I open the door
he'll ask for you.
I'd like to take him to your room
to see the bed with sheets
all white and clean and ironed,
we changed them every week,
I'd like him to see the dolls and the mirror
and the letters on the night table.
but it's not proper for me to do that,
it's the first time he's come to see you.
we'd better go right to the living-room
and I'll offer him some tea.
then I'll get the letters and his cards
as well.

you don't have to worry.
I'll be discreet, very discreet.
I won't ask his name
his profession.
we'll talk about you
only if he wants to
calmly
as if you were on a trip or expected home soon.

I'm old-fashioned, that's true,
and maybe I didn't understand you.

but you can be sure of this:
with a friend so loyal
I'll know how to behave.

before he leaves
I'll allow myself to ask for one favor
I'll ask him to keep writing
I hope you won't be angry
I hope I'm doing the right thing
to keep writing
every year
the same cards
the same words
as before.
I'll keep putting them
in order
in a little packet
on the night table.
I know that's not how one does
things,
I know it's not good breeding.
but you don't know how I like
to think the day will come
when we read
the September 4th cards
together
the two of us together and talking
beside your night table.

CHAINS

I've seen them outside in a car
four of them in that blue car on the street
smoking and
                    telling jokes
the whole night.
And then the telephone rings
                                             and it's always them.
The whole night
                          looking at them from behind the curtains
and the lights out so Mama wouldn't know.

The car showed up the first time
during the hunger strike.
It's not the same one that came
                                               for my sister.
They parked in front of the house
and the four of them took turns
                                                worked shifts
for three weeks.
The car shows up
                          now
every time Mama does something.
Tonight I'll see them again,
again the four of them smoking and
                                                       the telephone ringing.
The old lady bought a chain
                                          with forty other women
and again, once again, they'll chain themselves
                                                                    together.

Do you remember that judge
the one who refused to investigate
my sister's case?
Mama explained it to him, proved everything she had to
prove
I saw my daughter, sir, I saw her with my own eyes.
What else did she have to explain after that
to the judge?
My breasts hurt, mommy,
was all that my sister said,
and go away, go away
before they kill you.
And the judge said she was lying,
and that the word of an officer
in the Chilean Army
was worth more much much more
than a thousand of hers,
my beautiful sister her breasts
hurt that day
when the old lady finally found her
in that damned hospital.

That judge's house
has strong iron bars on the windows.
In the few minutes it takes
for the police to arrive
he'll have time to recognize the forty women,
recognize them one by one.
Time to understand
before he closes the curtains
the things my mother will do
to find the daughter they arrested
the year the month the day
when a blue car stops parking
in front of the door of her house
a car with four men.
And the phone doesn't ring
at three in the morning.

Then the judge will turn out the lights
and ask himself why nobody is coming to help him
and he will keep on looking and

looking and

looking

from behind every curtain

at the chain of mothers in the street.

They put the prisoner
against the wall.
A soldier ties his hands.
His fingers touch him—strong,
gentle, saying goodbye.
—Forgive me, compañero—
says the voice in a whisper.
The echo of his voice
and of
        those fingers on his arm
fills his body with light
        I tell you his body fills with light
and he almost does not hear
the sound of the shots.

PART 2

POEMS I WASN'T GOING TO SHOW ANYBODY

PROLOGUE: PARACHUTE

As for him
he can't afford the luxury of a breakdown.
He locks away his dreams
                                        and smiles bravely
and his roots
burn among ruins
                                        and he smiles bravely
for the camera that comes closer
and every adventure a color photograph
that tends to develop in black and white.

(As for me,
I can't afford the luxury of a breakdown.
I must go on
doing what I always do.
If I endlessly circle the deepest well,
if I pretend to plunge into fire,
if these feet test the vertigo of mud,
if black stars roar in my air,
don't worry.
Here it is, my favorite rope,
a secret anchor, a tattooed
                                        compass,
and water, water hidden in my hump.
I leap into the sun with darkness between my fingers,
with sure darkness against the sun,
that's how I leap
                              and for the plague
that grows and snarls on the road,

I have salves, spells, don't you see them?
I demand guarantees:
nothing must happen to me.)

He runs no risks, didn't I tell you?
He can't afford the luxury
of going out into silence,
of risking the blank look
of the deaf-mute
—the poor deaf-mute—
who left his safety cord at home.
And he doesn't want to find out
if beneath this infinite water
there is a bottom or more water.

Be careful.
Among flags and feet that come up from the rivers,
be careful with the sudden swamp of yourself.
Close up the sewer inside that makes you dizzy.
There's quicksand under the roots
of the best trees with the most blossoms.
Look: as day breaks
maybe the sun
is setting after all
for you.

BEGGAR

How would you like me to say it?
Save me, as Little Red Riding-Hood suggests?
Help, in the words of the Beatles?
Au secours, as the French say?
I have an old, vain heart,
and I will ask for nothing.
I will stay here just like the beggar
who was king of the spring
palace
and I hope that someone notices some day
before it is too late
that I'm dying with my hand out
an invisibly howling dead man
with my invisible hand held out.

And the one person who could see me,
see the silhouette of my fingers with his eyes,
is also awake and far away
in another kind of cage
sharing the corner of a blanket,
in a hut jammed with twenty other men,
and a guard who doesn't let him
out to breathe the night,
to fill himself with the relief of a Chilean summer night,
the cool, fragrant Chilean summer night,
as if the door locked on the outside
weren't enough
and the barbed wire beyond that
and the street patrols beyond that

and the walls inside all their heads beyond that
and the borders with dogs beyond that,
he could understand me.
What's happening to us is too real.

THERE IS NO WIND TO EASE THE FLOWERS

One day the blood in the pollen will put me to sleep,
the syllables of blood in the pollen will slowly put me to sleep.
The compañeros will come, they will say: and this one,
what happened to him, he used to be so strong.
It's so simple and so terrible and so me:
I was alone like a pond that irrigates the field,
a pond that gives water and breathes stars,
that no rivers come to,
where no children come
                                        to swim.
What happened to him, what could have happened to me?
I was turning into a knot with so much growing of arms,
with so much crossing of arms in search of other hands,
with so many impossible demands—all they demanded of me,
I satisfied them all.
The signs were there, don't say that in my stammerings,
in my secret, obvious telegrams,
I didn't explain everything.
None of you could decipher it
and now I survive like the hope of a land
                                                                        buried
in snow
in a wood where the sun freezes yellow.
One day I'm going to die slowly
I'm going to die of the blood in the pollen.

ST. GEORGE

I squandered mirrors the way some people get on trains
with the enthusiasm that some people feel when they bite
into an apple
so that the others could see their beautiful faces,
so that my friends could steal the lightning
from the sky
and keep it for the nights when everything is silence
and there are only clocks with broken alarms
that can't ring or shine in the dark
nights like now when I'm turned into a dead tree
in a dead bed.

Where are those mirrors?
Where did they go, why don't they return?
Where am I that I don't come to rescue me.
Killing dragons.
Or will I have to face the monsters
with crushed eyes and ruined lungs
and with the vague memory of what I did and will do
to guide me like a spider web
in the unending garden of death?

SOMETHING MORE THAN LIGHTBULBS

Unexplainable in the middle of the night,
a bird is singing
and sings and sings again.
Only I am listening to him.
Only I am awake
now when everybody
                                        is sleeping.
I am awake and alone.
My friends are not here,
my marriage is in trouble.
Now when I try to measure
if what I did
was good or bad,
when with every turn of the toboggan
the question comes back a child,
like a leaf that falls from the tree that is the same but older,
when I insist and insist again
that no one can hear me,
the bird continues
now as if no one were
hearing him either.
Perhaps he has confused my light
with the beginnings of dawn.
He sings, he wants company,
maybe he is happy that day
has come back sooner than he expected.
Wiser than me,
with his hundred times smaller brain,
so much wiser.

And I who can see no other light
than his song at night,
his song for me
because he thinks I'm the sun.
And now my son gets up
to pee.
Really, the night is full of dawns.
If I were not embalmed,
oh if I could only sing
certain that in the middle of this night
the sun
the sun
            is rising
somewhere near.

HABEAS CORPUS

sometimes I wake up in my when,
in my what do you call it I awake, in a maybe
that grieves me, that moves me
away from me,
sometimes I wake up in my absence,
and I can't avoid it,
I am nowhere,
awake in a burning field of ice
that lives, that floats, that breathes,
but just that, just
that.
do you remember the times we stayed up all night
getting ready for a trip
but now there are no suitcases or clothes,
and this time we don't leave at dawn,
I stay here saying good-bye to me
no ticket, no train.

I disappear and can't find me,
no light in the window shines in the night,
no nest,
I can't recognize me
in that mirror that doesn't exist.
But someone far away
demands my presence.

Closeby perhaps
someone offered help
and is looking for me in all the barracks,

they don't accept my death.
Only a great surge of solidarity
could make me present, could return me
to the world,
grow trees in me, arm me with something besides patience,
pull me out of the cold water I'm floating in,
demand that I exist again,
invent a yesterday for me, get me out of the basement
and find my shadow in the street,
there must be something like gravitational
universal love,
a law of human attraction,
the force of all the others operating closeby,
invisible hands that mold you in the darkness,
someone who dies for you,
who is born for me a little at a time
like the sun in love with its planet,
something that makes me
begin this interrupted
trip again
no suitcase, no clothes,
it's still hard for me to believe in it.

PART 3

UNDERTOW

PROLOGUE: THAT DEAFENING NOISE IS THE GARBAGE TRUCK

Today the cup broke;
how could I be so clumsy.

It made me very sad when it broke,
it was the one we had bought right after
we left the country,
one that we were fond of,
you could say it was almost
our friend,
bright red with white spots
for drinking café con leche
in the mornings,
those first mornings at the beginning.

So that there wouldn't be any slivers left,
any sharp bits to surprise us afterwards
in our soup, our feet, our eyelids,
I picked up all the tiny fragments
squatting
at first and then on all fours,
with the infinite care of a punished child
doing a chore over again
quietly, quietly,
and slowly.
We had it for
more than four years.

Today I broke a cup
and my exile began.

OCCUPATION ARMY

On this street corner in Santiago
—Huérfanos and Ahumada—
distance dries out and piles up.

Each time you pass by
—like a broken record
that someone tries to play
just one more time—
what we lived there leaps out
                    to hurt you,
everything you've had to forget
day by day.

That memory comes back to me too.
Slowly suddenly
                I am the echo of a record
that breaks and that is only played
                very very softly
whenever a train goes by.

In Santiago you go past that corner.
I cannot.

LAST WALTZ IN SANTIAGO

All that you've danced they take from you
they just take it
just like that.

They kill the dancer in you
they crush her slowly,
they skeleton, smoke,
before she can
                        dance this dance
                                    with you.

They break your rhumba, tango
                                                        they break you,
they dissolve your carnival in urine,
they put needles through the skin of your record,
they use the trumpet like a knife
                                                    and they shatter your violin
just like that.

They lock you in walls
that have no number,
among mirrors and songs covered with ashes,
they lock your hands, your feet, your collarbone,
and they tell you now dance you cripple
dance now you motherfucker,
they sentence you to tomb, they scrape you with sand.

let's dance, then,
my dear,

because they're taking away all that we've danced
—right now, listen to the footsteps coming closer
and someone is trying out shiny soldier's boots
right now—

right now.

SELF CRITICISM

Let's tell the truth once and for all:
we didn't recognize them.
But they were there
behind their military moustaches,
deep inside their medals,
an eye for an eye they were there,
a tooth for a tooth,
and we didn't know that we supplied the eyes
and they used sharp sticks,
we didn't know that the pulled teeth were ours
and the pliers were theirs.
Let's say that we were wrong: we
couldn't read their thoughts,
couldn't see the vein throbbing near the trigger,
couldn't hear the whipbeat of their hearts,
couldn't watch when they forced their wives
or told the orderly to bring coffee.

We didn't see that man when he knocked down the tree,
when he ejaculated into the pool,
when he swerved the car to run over
the child's ball.
Or did we see him, do we see him, did we know,
not want to see and know?
All we did was delay his appearance,
leave him in the labyrinth,
supposing he wouldn't escape,
that his real personality
was there forever,

lost among our words
and the lies and the peanuts
we threw to him.

His shadow appeared one day.
We thought it was an optical illusion.
Then the body appeared:
it was him, not just his shadow.

And tomorrow?

SOMETHING MUST BE HAPPENING TO MY ANTENNAS

I find myself crying at the end of General Hospital
I swear it's true
the worst soap opera on TV
the cheapest song
a good-bye on a platform
or a broken balloon in a child's hand
are all it takes
and I get a lump in my throat
my eyes burn like acid
my nose itches
my heart pounds
my breathing becomes irregular
maybe tears will come
and my eyes grow red

I know the tricks and techniques of the movies
I've studied how the violins manipulate us
I spent my life denouncing Doris Day

but during General Hospital
something clouds over inside
and something wet and salty runs down my cheeks

I'm like a stone when I receive the news of your death
lists of crippled people come off the plane
your best friend limping
I learn that they killed your sister on a street corner
the children in the slums eat cats and dogs
if they can find them

you haven't worked for fifteen months
another worker clubbed
the noise of a stick on a shoulder

and I am not moved
I am not moved
        I must be very sick
I'm afraid
I'm afraid
        I'm afraid of what's happening to me
I'm afraid
        so afraid
        of what's happening to me

THE TELEPHONE. LONG DISTANCE.
BAD NEWS, SAYS A FAMILIAR VOICE.
WE HAVE TO ORGANIZE A CAMPAIGN.

and if it were you?
and if this time
it were you?

before they say anything
before they add a single word
like a cat that walks through darkness
your memory cuts through me
like a kick
it cuts through me
your body
like a white cat that walks and shatters
the darkness

but it's another name, it's another
name.
suddenly
everything lasts suddenly
stiff and twisted
like nails in the suddenly so close
hand
I am flooded with
the lonely horror of relief
because it isn't
you.

How can I feel
this unspeakable relief
like cats

dirty cats
that I smother so I don't have to look at them,
how can I feel this relief
because this time
it isn't
you?

I write down the facts carefully. I hang up the phone and begin to call the newspapers one by one to give them the name of the compañero who has been arrested, the name of the compañero I don't know.

THE TELEPHONE. LONG DISTANCE. BAD NEWS.

And this time?
who is it
this time?
start to make plans
this time and the next
time
learn to develop
contacts
differentiate
use
contacts
measure how much space
less and less space
is left in the newspaper
contacts
keep up contacts
like other people put away preserves
or their favorite clothes
or wine in a good cellar
for another day
and other phone calls
for friends
who haven't been caught yet
relatives compañeros compañeras fighters
who haven't been caught yet
contacts
learn not to abuse
my
goddamn contacts

Do you know something?
We rank the life
and death
of others
as easily as we used to
make shopping lists
for the week.

may god have mercy on us.

I write down the facts carefully. I hang up the phone and begin to call the newspapers one by one to give them the name of the compañero who has been arrested, the name of the compañero I don't know.

MANEUVERS

I've always written from the shore,
from the eternal approaching shore
that anyone can set up like a tent in a desert
or a beach without an island in the middle of the sea.

I know,
the ebb and flow have little to say to the sea,
everyone knows that.

Even though waves and fish come,
even though bottles or boats go,
even though ports and precipices and reefs,
with so much changing of tides at the docks
the ocean is not interested
in the coastline where water and rock dispute
their small, antiquated drop of supremacy.

Compared to huge weights, underwater kingdoms,
cataclysms ready to explode, abysses
that are the birth of the moon,
the depths where garbage dissolves,
the roar that brought the first mollusk out of the volcano,
what can this shore matter where I am writing
this cloth without a table where I decide to eat.
But don't misunderstand me.
This isn't the only sound I make.
Look at the naked feet.
Is it wrong to sing of something as simple
as shoes?

Should we forget the hollow of the torn-out tongue?
If it is dark shall we cease to praise
the rising sun?
Look at that hand in another hand.
Without the fist that denounces and never doubts,
the slender fingers
that should be playing Bach
cannot survive.
Look at the hollow of the torn-out tongue.
Look at the naked feet.
Look at the slender fingers
groping in the garbage
for the day before yesterday's first meal.
Are we never to say we shall
Are we never to say we shall fight
the good fight

And yet I will always know what it is to live not sleeping,
not entirely awake,
like a dream that the sea turns into skin
like this, on the wing of the life that flies, like this, just like
this,

it isn't easy, let me tell you,
to be an island of water in the middle of the sea.

VOCABULARY

1

But how can I tell their story
if I was not there?

When two of them met
far away
on an unfamiliar street corner
they could not know if it was
a first meeting
or a farewell.
They could not know who was looking at them
from the quadrangle
of that window.
Reporting every movement
every movement of their lips.

I was looking at them from another country
and I cannot tell their story.
I was calling from another country
and the phone was always busy.

2

Show me a word I can use.
Show me one verb.
An adjective as clear as a ray of light.
Listen carefully to the bottom of every sentence,
to the attic and the dust in the furniture
of every sentence,

perk up your ears,
listen and look under the bed
of every sentence
at the soldiers waiting their turn
at the foot
of the bride's bed.

To preserve just one word.
What is it to be?
Like a question on a quiz show.
If you could take one word with you
to the future,
what is it to be?

Find it.
Plunge into the garbage heap.
Stick your hands deep into the ooze.
Close your fist around the fragment of a mirror
fractured by feet that dance on what should have been
a wedding night.

Let me tell you something.
Even if I had been there
I could not have told their story.

3

I was calling from another country
and the phone was still busy.
I was trying to call home
and the machine had just swallowed
my last dime.

4

As for the story I cannot tell.
They accumulated tenderness
as others accumulate money.

Ask them.
Even if the phone is busy.
Even if the machine has just swallowed your last dime.

Even if the operator drowns out all the other voices.
Ask them for the verse our lovers will still need
if we are ever again to bathe
                                        in the same river.

Let them speak for themselves.

EPILOGUE

PROBLEMS WITH DOORS

Of course it endures, hard
and dark and closes

one door after another
during the entire mass
production by hands
that don't see light not light

one door after another
locked lock the entire night
there goes the shadow of the guard outside
inside the eye of the prisoner who does not
sleep

and the bunch of keys
of course in the hand
of that shadow who doesn't give in
who walks and watches

and enduring still in other locks
in the during hardening
the ear of the woman waiting
for the steps of the husband
who is not hers
and who never arrives

one lock after another
during the entire mass
production by hands

that don't see light not light
not even the one
            that goes out
                        and does not endure

and hardening still in other durings
while the child who wakes up
                              in the room without doors
very inside this thing that endures and endures and does not
                                                            end
and someone
            someone enduring
            that shadow that walks and watches
                                            and doesn't give in
has just locked the last window
enclosed the sun between a nail and half a finger
            inside the eye of the prisoner who does not sleep
            there goes the shadow of the guard who grows
                                                            dark

there is the key
            make the hand
            that produces all night long
            make the hand
            fill up with doorways

there it is didn't I tell you
there it is there
              it is
                  the key
of course clearly